THE UNDERBURY WITCHES

John Connolly   )68. He is
the author of (>ery *Dead*
Thing and *Blac*   *The Book*
of Lost Things, \

All royalties fr   ie Open
Door series go   s choice.
The Underbury \   retstown
Gang Camp, B: dare.

NEW ISLAND Open Door

THE UNDERBURY WITCHES
Published 2006
by New Island
2 Brookside
Dundrum Road
Dublin 14

www.newisland.ie

A CIP catalogue record for this book is available from the British Library

ISBN 1 905494 01 7

New Island receives financial assistance from
The Arts Council (An Chomhairle Ealaíon), Dublin, Ireland.

Typeset by New Island
Printed in Ireland by ColourBooks
Cover design by Artmark

1 3 5 4 2

Dear Reader,

On behalf of myself and the other contributing authors, I would like to welcome you to the fifth Open Door series. We hope that you enjoy the books and that reading becomes a lasting pleasure in your life.

Warmest wishes,

Patricia Scanlan.

Patricia Scanlan
Series Editor

One

Steam and fog swirled upon the station platform at Underbury. It turned men and women to grey ghosts. It created traps out of cases and chests. The night was growing colder. A faint layer of frost could already be seen upon the ticket-office roof. In the waiting room, people stayed close to the old radiators that smelled of burnt dust. Some drank tea from cheap cups and ate stale buns from cracked plates. Tired children cried in the arms of weary parents. An old man tried to talk to two soldiers in uniform. The soldiers were on their way to France, and maybe death, so were in no mood to talk. The old man gave up.

The stationmaster's whistle rang in the gloom. He swung his lamp high above his head and the train slowly began to move away. It left two other men standing on the platform. The new arrivals did not belong in Underbury. They carried heavy bags and wore city clothes. One was larger and older than the other. He wore a bowler hat on his head. A scarf covered his mouth and chin. His brown coat was worn at the sleeves. His shoes were built for comfort alone.

The other man was shorter. His coat was long and black. He wore no hat. His eyes were very blue. He might almost have been called handsome, in the right light.

"No one to welcome us, then, sir," said the older man. His name was Arthur

Stokes. He was proud to be a sergeant of detectives in the greatest police force in the world at Scotland Yard.

"The locals never like to accept help from London," said the other policeman. His name was Burke. He was an inspector. "One of us would be bad enough. Two must be more than they can stand."

They made their way through the station to the road outside. A man stood waiting beside an old black car.

"You'll be the men from London," he said.

"We are," said Burke. "And who might you be?"

"My name is Croft. The constable sent me to collect you. He's busy at the moment. The newspapers keep calling him."

Burke looked angry. "He was told not to talk to the press until we got here," he said.

Croft reached out to take their bags.

"He has to talk to them to tell them he can't talk to them, doesn't he?" he said.

Croft winked at Burke. Sergeant Stokes had never seen anyone wink at the inspector before. He wasn't sure that Croft was the best person to try it.

"Fair point, sir," said Sergeant Stokes quickly. They had only been in the village for ten minutes. He didn't want a fight just yet.

"Whose side are you on, sergeant?" said Burke.

"The side of law and order, sir," said Stokes. "The side of law and order."

*

The witch panic gripped Europe for over three hundred years. It began in the mid-1400s. It ended with Anna Goldi's death in Switzerland in 1782. She was the last woman in Western

Europe to be executed for witchcraft. The executions took the lives of between fifty and one hundred thousand people. Most were women, and most of them were old and poor. It was 1736 before the crime of witchcraft was removed from the books of law in England. That was almost one hundred and twenty years after the deaths of the three women known as the Underbury Witches.

Two

Croft drove the two policemen into the village of Underbury. They took a pair of small but warm rooms in the Vintage Inn. They ate some food, and then the two detectives were brought to the local undertaker's. The village doctor, Allinson, was waiting there for them. Constable Waters, the village policeman, was with him. Allinson was young. He walked with a slight limp due to childhood polio. It meant that he could not serve with the army in France. Waters, in Burke's view, was the usual village copper. He was slow, but not careful, and thought that he was smarter than he really was. The undertaker showed them the body that lay upon his slab.

The body was that of a man in his early forties. His face was grey. The men could smell the decay on him. There were long cuts across his face and more cuts on his chest and belly. The wounds were deep and went far into his body. His insides were visible to them.

"His name was Malcolm Trevors," said Waters. "Mal to most people. Single man, no family."

"Good Lord," said Stokes. "It looks like an animal attacked him."

Burke told the undertaker that he could go. The little man left without a word. Once the door was closed behind him, Burke turned to the doctor.

"You've examined him?" he asked

Allinson shook his head. "Not fully. I took a look at those cuts, though."

"And?"

"If it's the work of an animal, it's like none I've ever seen."

"Why do you say that?"

The doctor leaned over the body of the dead man. He pointed to smaller marks to the left and right of the main cuts.

"You see these? I'd say they were left by thumbs with deep fingernails."

He held up his hand and curled his fingers as though holding a ball. He raked them through the air.

"The deep cuts came from the fingers. The smaller cuts came from the thumbs," he said.

Burke leaned over the body. He looked closely at the hands.

"Can you pass me a thin blade?" he asked.

Allinson took a scalpel from his bag. He handed it to Burke. Burke stuck the blade under the nail of one of the dead man's fingers.

"Get me a bowl."

Allinson gave him a small glass dish. Burke scraped something into it from under the nail. He did the same thing with each of the dead man's fingers. When he was done, a small pile of stuff lay upon the dish.

"What is it?" asked Constable Waters.

"Tissue," said Allinson. "Skin, not fur. Very little blood."

"He fought back," said Burke. "He cut his attacker."

"He'll be long gone, then," said Waters. "A man marked in that way won't hang around to be found out."

"No, perhaps not," said Burke. "Still, it's something. Can you take us to where the body was found?"

"Now?" said Waters.

"No, the morning should do. It's too

dark now. Doctor, when do you think you might know more?"

Allinson began to roll up his sleeves.

"I'll start straight away, if you like. I'll talk to you tomorrow."

Burke looked to his sergeant.

"Right then," he said. "We'll be off for now. We'll see you at nine in the morning. Thank you, gentlemen."

And with that, the strangers left.

★

Only five hundred people lived in the village of Underbury. Once upon a time, there were many more. The witch trials changed that.

Five children had died in the space of a single week. They were all firstborn males. The villagers suspected three women who were new in the village. The women said they were sisters from London. The eldest, Ellen Drury, was a midwife. She helped other women give birth. She had taken over from Grace Polley, who had drowned. Ellen Drury had delivered the male children who had died. It was said that she had cursed them. But it was mostly the men who said it. They were afraid of Ellen Drury and her sisters. They were strong women. They spoke their mind. They gave other women ideas. The deaths of the children gave the men an excuse to deal with the sisters. They sent a message about them to London, calling them witches. The king sent a pair of witchfinders from London to look into the matter.

The Drury sisters were tortured. Another young girl, under threat of torture, said that she had seen Ellen Drury make the poison that killed the children. On 18 November 1628, Ellen Drury and her sisters were hanged in Underbury. Ellen Drury was the last to die. She kept staring at the men of the village, even as she dangled from the end of the rope. Finally, a man threw oil on her and set her on fire. The bodies were buried in a hole outside the graveyard.

Nobody spoke of them again.

Three

Dr Allinson worked all night. He met Burke and Stokes for breakfast the next morning. He told them that the deepest wound went from the man's belly all the way to his heart. The heart had been pierced in five places by long claws or nails.

"Are you telling us that a hand was pushed up through this man's body?" asked Burke.

"It would seem so," said the doctor. "It is no easy thing to tear apart a man in such a way. The nails of the hand must have been very strong. The fingers may have been added to in some way. Perhaps metal claws, which could be put on or taken off as needed, were used."

The doctor was very tired. His wife arrived to take him home. Her name was Emily. She was tall and blonde with flawed green eyes.

"I'm sorry that I could not be of more help," said Allinson. "I will look at the body again tonight, before he is buried. I may have missed something."

Burke thanked him. The doctor stepped outside. His wife was behind him. Burke moved aside to let her pass.

And a strange thing happened.

A mirror hung on the wall across from Burke. He could see himself reflected in it. He could also see Emily Allinson. But it looked as if her reflection moved more slowly than she did. The reflection seemed to turn its face toward Burke, even though the woman herself did not. That face, for an instant, was not that of Emily Allinson. It was black and ruined. Its mouth hung open and its skin was burnt. The eyes were like cinders in their sockets. Then Emily Allinson went outside and the vision was gone.

Burke watched Mrs Allinson walk her husband down the street. The doctor leaned on her for support. He was the only man on the street. There were few men under the age of forty in Underbury. Most were off fighting in France. Many would not come back. It would be a long time before places like Underbury found some balance again between men and women.

Burke went back to his sergeant. But he did not eat the rest of his breakfast.

"Anything wrong, sir?" asked Stokes.

"Just tired," said Burke.

Stokes nodded. He mopped up the runny egg yolk with his toast. It was a good breakfast, he thought. But not as good as the breakfasts his wife cooked for him. She often said that Inspector Burke could do with a little fattening up. Stokes knew that by "fattening up" his wife meant that Burke should be married, with a wife to cook him meals. Inspector Burke had little time for women, though. He lived alone with his books and his cat. He was a little uncomfortable with women. But Stokes was fond of Inspector Burke. He was a very good copper indeed. Stokes was proud to serve with him. Inspector Burke's private life was a matter for himself and no one else. That was what Stokes thought. His wife did not agree.

Burke stood up and took his coat from a hook on the wall.

"I think we need some air," he said.

"It's time to see where Mal Trevors died."

Burke and Stokes stood at one side of the fence post. Constable Waters stood at the other. They could still see traces of the victim's blood upon the wood. Pieces of his clothing were caught in the barbed wire of the fence. Beyond lay open fields, then the low wall around the church and the graveyard.

"He was found against the post," said Waters. "His arms were hanging on the wire."

"Who found him?" asked Stokes.

"Fred Paxton. He lives on the next farm. He said Trevors left the pub shortly before ten. Paxton left an hour later."

"Did he touch the body?"

"No need to. He knew Trevors was dead."

"We'll have to talk to Paxton."

"Thought you might say that. He and his missus live not half a mile up the road. I told them to expect us this morning."

"Did you search the area?" Burke asked.

"I did."

Burke waited. Trevors was crossing the field when he was attacked. It had been a cold night. It had not grown any warmer. Whoever had attacked Trevors must have left some tracks upon the grass.

"Well?"

"There were only two sets of footprints: Mal Trevors's and Fred Paxton's."

"Perhaps he was attacked on the road," said Stokes. "He was trying to escape across the fields and died on the fence."

"I don't think so," said Waters. "There was no blood between the road and the fence. I checked."

Burke knelt and looked at the ground. There was still a lot of dried blood on the grass. If what Waters said was true, then Trevors had been attacked on this spot. And he had died here.

"Something must have been missed," he said at last. "Whoever killed Trevors didn't pop out of thin air. We'll go over the ground, inch by inch. There has to be some trail."

The three men spread out from the death post. Burke moved toward the cemetery. Stokes headed for the road. Waters walked toward the Paxtons' farm. They searched for an hour but found nothing. It seemed that Mal Trevors had been attacked out of nowhere.

Burke finished first. He sat upon the low cemetery wall and watched the others. In his heart, Burke knew that it was a waste of time. A proper search needed more men. But there were no men to call. Still, it made no sense to him that a big man like Trevors could be killed in this way.

Burke was sweating, despite the cold. He was starting to feel a little ill. It's this place, he thought. It saps your energy. Underbury was a village emptied of its best men. They were all now fighting in far-off fields. Those who were left behind were old or weak. It had changed the village. Burke could feel it. It was changing him too.

Burke went to rejoin the other policemen. As he did so, his foot hit a stone. He knelt down and brushed the tips of his fingers along the ground. There was a slab there, almost hidden by long grass and weeds. There was no writing on the stone, but Burke knew what it was. Someone had been buried here, someone not worthy of holy ground.

He saw two other slabs nearby. One had been broken recently. Someone had taken a hammer to it. There was a hole as big as Burke's fist at the centre. Burke slipped two fingers into the gap. He could feel no earth below. There was just empty space. He tied his pen to a piece of thread and fed it through the gap. Again, nothing. The hole beneath was very deep. There was no earth.

Strange, he thought.

He stood up. Stokes and Waters were watching him from the road. He walked back to them. Waters said that now was the time to talk to the Paxtons. They could take some tea there for their trouble.

"What kind of man was Trevors?" Burke asked Waters.

"I didn't care much for him myself," said Waters. "He served time in a prison up north for assault. He came back down here when he was released. He lived with his father until the old man died. After that, it was just him alone on that farm."

"And the mother?"

"Died when Mal was a boy. Her husband used to beat her, they say. I think Mal had some of his old man's bad habits. He was jailed for beating up a – well, you'll forgive me, sir, a prostitute in Manchester. Near killed her, from what I hear. When he came back here, he took up with a woman named Elsie Warden. She got rid of him when he fell back into his old ways with her. Her family gave Mal a beating to teach him a lesson. A week ago, he went to her house in the night and tried to speak to her. Her father and younger brothers sent him on his way. They'd already given him a taste of his own medicine once. He didn't fancy another spoonful."

Burke and Stokes looked at each other.

"Could the Wardens be suspects?" said Burke.

"They were all in the bar when Trevors left. They were still there when Fred Paxton came back after finding the body. They never left. Even Elsie was with them. They're in the clear."

Waters took a sheet of paper from his pocket. He gave it to Burke.

"Thought you might want this. It's a list of all the people who were in the bar that night. A star marks the ones who were there from the time Trevors left until the body was found."

Burke took the list and read it. One name caught his eye.

"Mrs Allinson was there that night?"

"And her husband. Saturday night's the big night in the village. Most people find their way to the inn, sooner or later."

Emily Allinson's name was one of those marked with a star.

"And she never left," Burke said, so quietly that nobody heard him utter the words.

Four

The Paxtons were a young couple with no children. Fred was born about twenty miles west of Underbury. He lived in London for a time. Then he came back to Underbury with his new wife. They fed the detectives bread and cheese and brewed up a big pot of tea.

"I was walking along, my mind on getting home," said Fred Paxton. He was blind in one eye. His left eye was yellowy-white, with lines of red mixed in. It brought an image back to Burke from when he was a boy. He had gone on a visit to his uncle's farm in the country. There, his father had drunk milk fresh from the cow. The boy had seen blood in the creamy liquid.

"There was a shape at the fence," Paxton went on. "It looked like a scarecrow. But there's no scarecrow on that land. I climbed the gate and went to have a look. I never saw so much blood. I felt it under my boots. I'd say Mal wasn't dead long when I found him."

"Why do you say that?" asked Stokes.

"His insides were steaming," said Paxton simply.

"What did you do then?" said Burke.

"I went back to the village, fast as I could. I ran into the pub and told old Ken the barman to send for the constable. When all was done, I went home to the missus here."

Burke turned to Mrs Paxton. She had spoken just five words since their arrival. She was a slight thing, with dark hair and large blue eyes. She was quite beautiful.

"Can you add to what your husband has told us, Mrs Paxton?" he asked her. "Did you hear or see anything that might help us?"

Her voice was very low. Burke had to lean forward to hear what she was saying.

"I was asleep in bed when Fred came in," she said. "When he told me it was Mal Trevors, well, I just felt something turn inside me. It was terrible."

She rose from the table. Burke watched her go, then caught himself doing so. He returned his attention to the men around him.

"How did people take the news of Mal Trevors's death?" Burke asked Paxton.

"They were shocked, I suppose," he said.

"Was Elsie Warden shocked?"

"Well, she was later, when she found out," said Paxton.

"Later?"

"Elsie was taken ill at the bar not long before I got back. The doctor's wife took care of her in old Ken's kitchen."

Burke asked if he might use the toilet. Fred Paxton told him it was outside. He offered to show him. But Burke told him that he would be able to find it. He walked through the kitchen and found the privy in the garden. He relieved himself while he thought. When he went back outside, Mrs Paxton was standing at the kitchen window. Her upper body was bare. She was washing herself with a cloth from the sink. She stopped when she saw him. Her breasts were exposed to him. Her body was very white. Burke looked at her for just a second longer. Slowly she turned away, her back pale against the shadows. Burke went around the side of the house to avoid the kitchen. Upon his return, Waters and Stokes stood and the four men walked out together. Paxton spoke to Waters about local matters. Stokes stood on the road, taking the air.

Suddenly, Burke found Mrs Paxton by his side.

"I'm sorry," he said. "I didn't mean to startle you while you were washing."

She blushed slightly.

"It wasn't your fault," she said.

"I do have just one other question," he said to her.

She waited.

"Did you like Mal Trevors?"

It took a moment for her to answer.

"No, sir," she said at last. "I did not."

"May I ask why?"

"He was a brute of a man. I saw the

way he looked at me. Our land was next to his. I made a point never to be alone in the fields when he was around."

"Did you tell your husband this?"

"No, but he knew how I felt."

She stopped talking suddenly. She was aware that she might have said something to get her husband, or herself, into trouble.

"It's all right, Mrs Paxton," said Burke. "You and your husband are not suspects here."

"So you say."

"Listen to me. Whoever killed Mal Trevors was big and strong. With respect, you are not. The killer would have been covered in blood after what was done to Trevors. Your husband was not. You see?"

"Yes, thank you," she replied. "Fred is a good man."

Burke was still not sure that she believed him.

"But you felt shocked at Trevors's death, even if you didn't like him," said Burke.

Again, there was a pause before the reply came. Burke could see her husband coming to his wife's aid. There was little time left.

"I wished that he was dead," said Mrs Paxton softly. "The day before he died, he brushed against me when we were in Mr Little's store. He did it on purpose. I felt him push into me. I felt his … *thing*. He was a pig. I was tired of being afraid to walk in our own fields. So, for a moment, I wished him dead. Then a day later he was dead. I suppose I wondered …"

"If somehow you might have caused his death?"

"Yes."

Fred Paxton was now beside them.

"Is everything all right, love?" he asked, placing an arm around his wife's shoulders.

"Everything's fine, now," she said.

She smiled at her husband. It calmed him, and Burke caught a glimpse of the real power behind their marriage. There was strength hidden inside this small, pretty woman.

And he felt a surge of unease.

Everything's fine.

Everything's fine now that Mal Trevors is dead.

Sometimes, you do *get what you wish for, don't you, my love?*

Five

By now it was growing dark. Constable Waters said that it would not be wise to visit Elsie Warden's family after dusk.

"They're an uneasy lot," he said. "The old man will have a shotgun in his hand to greet visitors at this hour."

The three men went back to the village. Stokes and Burke ate stew together in a corner of the inn. Nobody spoke to them. They were not wanted in this place. Burke decided to visit Dr Allinson. He wanted some time alone, so he told Stokes to stay at the inn. Stokes, who liked the idea of a quiet, warm pint by the fire, agreed. Burke took a lamp from the inn, then set out to walk to the Allinsons' house. It lay about one mile north of the village. It was a starless night, and Burke was glad of the lamp.

All of the windows were dark when he arrived at the house, except for one. He knocked loudly and waited. After some minutes, Mrs Allinson opened the door to him. She wore a very formal blue dress that hung from her neck to her ankles. It looked dated to Burke's eye. But she carried it off. She was helped by her height and her fine features. Her flawed green eyes glinted with amusement.

"Inspector Burke, this is a surprise," she said. "My husband had not told me to expect you."

"I had not told him I was coming," said Burke. "Is he at home?"

Mrs Allinson asked Burke to step

inside. He followed her into the drawing-room, where Mrs Allinson lit the lamps.

"I'm afraid he was called out. He should not be very long. May I offer you tea?"

Burke thanked her, but refused. Mrs Allinson sat down on a couch. She waved Burke toward an armchair.

"I was surprised that you opened the door yourself," he said. "I thought you would have a maid to do it."

"I gave her the night off," said Mrs Allinson. "Her name is Elsie Warden. She's a local girl. Have you met Elsie, Inspector?"

Burke said that he had not.

"You'll like her," said Mrs Allinson. "A lot of men seem to like Elsie."

Once again, Burke was aware of Mrs Allinson's amusement. He knew that it was at his expense. He just did not yet know why.

"I hear that you were with her on the night Mal Trevors died."

Mrs Allinson raised her left eyebrow slowly. There was also the hint of a smile on the left side of her mouth. It was as though a wire ran from eye to jaw, linking the way that they moved.

"I was 'with' my husband, Inspector," she replied.

"Do you usually spend your Saturday nights at the village inn?"

"You sound like you don't approve, Inspector. Don't you believe that ladies should be out with their husbands? Doesn't your wife spend time with you away from the house?"

"I'm not married."

"That is a shame," said Mrs Allinson. "I believe that a wife tames a man. She improves him. A good woman can make gold from the lead of most men."

"Was Mal Trevors a man of lead?" asked Burke. "Could he have been improved?"

"Mal Trevors was bad metal," said Mrs Allinson. "In my view, he is of more use to the earth lying beneath it than he ever was when he walked upon it. He will provide food for worms and for plants. Poor eating, but better than none at all that."

Burke did not reply. Few people seemed to have a good word to say about the dead man. Still, Burke had to do all in his power to track down his killer. Even bad men had the right to justice.

"We were talking about Miss Elsie Warden," he said. "I was told she fell ill on the night that Mal Trevors died."

"She was sick," said Mrs Allinson. "I took care of her as best I could."

"May I ask the cause?"

"You may ask Elsie Warden if you choose. It is not my place to tell you such things."

"Elsie Warden clearly trusts you a great deal," said Burke.

Mrs Allinson tilted her head. She looked at Burke in a new way. She was like a cat watching a mouse trying to escape, even though its tail was trapped under the cat's paw.

"Elsie is a strong young woman," said Mrs Allinson. "This is not a village that likes strong women. Those who are strong need to support one another."

"I don't understand," said Burke.

"They hanged witches here many years ago," said Mrs Allinson. "Three women died at the heart of the village. They are still known as the Underbury Witches. Their bodies lie buried beyond the graveyard walls."

"The three stones," said Burke.

"So you have seen them?"

"I didn't know who lay there. I just knew that they were graves of some kind."

"A cross is carved under each stone, facing down," said Mrs Allinson. "It is supposed to keep the witches from rising again. Even in death, they were feared."

"How do you know about the crosses?"

"I read it in the village records."

"But this is the twentieth century. Underbury is not like that now."

"Really? I beg to differ. You must have heard what Mal Trevors was like. He was foul, and there are others like him. Underbury is still the same. Men do not change."

Burke shrugged.

"I never met him, except to look upon his body," he said. "All I know is what others tell me."

"Why are you not married, Inspector?" asked Mrs Allinson suddenly. "Why is there no woman in your life?"

"My job takes up much of my time," he began. "Perhaps I have never met the right woman."

Mrs Allinson leaned forward.

"I suspect," she said, "that there is no 'right' woman for you. I don't think that you like women, Inspector. I don't mean in the physical sense. I am sure that you have lusts like most men have. I mean that you don't like their minds. You distrust them. You don't understand them. That makes you fear them. They are alien to you. And you are afraid of them for that reason. You are just like the men of Underbury who wanted those women hanged."

"I'm not afraid of women, Mrs

Allinson," said Burke. He tried to sound calm, but his voice broke a little.

Burke heard footsteps. The front door opened. The doctor called to his wife. Burke did not move. He found himself staring only at Mrs Allinson, caught in the depths of those green eyes.

"Really, Inspector, I don't know if that's true," she said. "In fact, I don't believe that's true at all."

Dr Allinson joined them. After a short time, his wife took her leave of them.

"I'll be seeing you again, Inspector," she said. "I look forward to it."

Burke spent an hour with Allinson. The doctor had nothing new to tell. Still, Burke enjoyed trading ideas back and forth. Allinson offered to take him back to the village. Burke said that he would rather walk. He thought better when he was alone. He drank a little brandy to warm him on the journey, then left the house.

The brandy was a mistake. It clouded his head. And the cold did little to sober him. He almost slipped before he even made it to the road. From then on he kept to the middle. He was afraid of falling into a ditch.

After a time, he heard a sound from the bushes to his right. He stopped and listened. Whatever was in the bushes also stopped. Burke was a man of the city. He did not know what kind of animal might be lying in the dark. Perhaps it was a badger or a fox. He moved on, the lamp raised, and something ran behind him. It brushed past his coat as it went. He turned quickly. He saw a flash of black as the creature ran into the bushes to his left.

It had crossed the road behind his back. It had come so close that it had touched him as it went.

Burke brushed at his coat. His fingers came back covered in black pieces. They looked like burnt paper. He peered at them in the lamplight. Then he lifted them to his nose to sniff them.

They smelled of burning, but not of paper. Burke had once entered a house that was on fire. He had found only one person alive. It was a woman, and her body was already badly burnt. Pieces of her skin had stuck to Burke's hands. The smell of it had never left him. It was why he never ate pork. Pork smelled like roasted human meat. And that was the smell that now lay upon his fingers.

He tried to rub it away on his coat. He started walking faster. His shoes made a slapping sound on the road. All the time, he felt himself being followed behind the bushes. At last he came to the village. He felt the creature in the bushes stop before the first house. Burke was breathing heavily. He paused and stared into the darkness. He thought for an instant that he saw a darker shape within it. A figure waited in the shadows. But it was gone almost as soon as he saw it. Its shape stayed with him, though. He saw it in his dreams that night: the curve of its hips, the swelling of its breasts.

It was the shape of a woman.

Six

The next morning, Waters drove Stokes and Burke to the Warden family's farm. Burke was quiet on the journey. He did not speak of the night before. He had slept badly. The stink of burnt meat seemed to cling to his pillow. Once he awoke to the sound of tapping at his window. When he went to check, all was still and silent outside. Yet he could have sworn that the smell of roasted flesh was stronger at the glass. He dreamed of Mrs Paxton. She watched him through the glass with her breasts bare. But in his dream her face became that of Mrs Allinson. The green of her eyes had turned to the black of cinders.

Elsie Warden's young brothers were out in the fields. Her father was away for the day. Only Elsie and her mother were home when the policemen arrived. Burke knew that there was bad blood between the Warden family and the late Mal Trevors. Mrs Warden, though, would not answer his questions. She kept looking out of the window, hoping her sons would arrive and get rid of the policemen. She stayed sullen and silent. Elsie Warden was more open. Burke was surprised at how confident she was. She had grown up in a house full of men. But she was not like her mother. She did not need men to stand up for her.

"We were all in the pub that evening," she told Burke. "Me, my mum and dad, and my brothers. All of us. That's the way around here. Saturday nights are special."

"But you knew Mal Trevors?"

"He tried to court me," she said. Her eyes dared Burke to find a reason why this should not be so. The detective was not about to argue with her. Elsie Warden had lush dark hair and gypsy looks. Sergeant Stokes was trying hard not to look at her body.

"And did you respond?"

Elsie Warden looked coy.

"Whatever do you mean by that?" she asked.

Burke felt himself redden. Stokes took a fit of coughing.

"I meant –" Burke began. He was not sure now what he *had* meant. Stokes came to the rescue.

"What the inspector means, miss, is did you like Mal Trevors? Or was he barking up the wrong tree, so to speak?"

"Ah," said Elsie. "I liked him well enough, to begin with."

"She always liked bad sorts," said her mother.

She kept her head down as she spoke. She did not look at her daughter. Burke wondered if the old woman was scared of her. Elsie Warden was full of life and energy. She was all that her mother was not.

"Was Mal Trevors a bad sort?" asked Burke.

Elsie tried the coy look again. It did not work this second time.

"I think you know what Mal Trevors was," she said.

"Did he hurt you?"

"He tried."

"What happened?"

"I hit him, and I ran."

"And then?"

"He came looking for me."

"And took a beating for his troubles," said Burke.

"I don't know anything about that," she said.

Burke nodded. He took his notebook from his pocket. He flicked through the pages. He was pleased to see Elsie Warden crane her neck slightly. She was trying to see what was written in the notebook. Burke hid the page with his hand. It was blank. But he did not want her to know that. He wanted to make her nervous. It was working.

"I'm told you took ill the night Mal Trevors was killed," he said.

Elsie Warden blinked hard. It was a small reaction, but enough for Burke. He waited for her to speak. He watched as Elsie thought about the answers she might give. Burke felt a change in her. He was aware of the charm slowly leaving her. It slipped from her body and dripped through the cracks in the floor. Something else replaced it. It looked like anger.

"That's true," she said softly. Her lips were very tight.

"Before or after you heard about Mal Trevors?"

"Before."

"May I ask what made you ill?"

"You may ask," she said. "You will embarrass yourself."

"I'll take that chance," said Burke.

"I had my visitor," she said. "The monthly guest. Are you happy now?"

Burke gave no sign of happiness or unhappiness.

"And Mrs Allinson helped you?"

"She did. She tended to me. Then she took me home later."

"It must have been very bad for you to have needed her help."

He was aware of a sharp intake of breath from Waters.

"Now, sir, don't you think we've gone far enough?" he asked.

Burke stood.

"For the moment," he said.

He began to walk, then seemed to trip over a chair leg. He fell against Elsie Warden, then used the wall to hold himself up. Stokes came to his aid.

"Are you all right, sir?" he asked.

Burke waved him away.

"I'm fine," he said. "I just felt a little weak."

Elsie Warden now had her back to him.

"I'm sorry, miss," said Burke. "I hope I didn't hurt you."

Elsie shook her head. She turned to face him. Burke thought she was a little paler than before. Her hands were folded across her chest.

"No," she said. "You didn't."

The three men prepared to leave. Mrs Warden saw them to the door.

"You're a rude man," she said to Burke. "My husband will hear of this."

"I don't doubt it," he replied. "I should tend to your daughter if I were you. She looks ill."

He said nothing to Stokes or Waters as they drove back to the village. Instead, he thought of Elsie Warden. He saw again the look of pain that crossed her face as he fell against her body.

And the drops of fresh blood upon her blouse that were almost hidden by her folded arms.

Seven

Mal Trevors was buried the next day. Many people came to his funeral. He was not liked, but a funeral gave them a chance to meet and talk. Burke stood by the fresh grave and watched them all. The Wardens were there. The men made their dislike of Burke clear through their looks. But they did not confront him. The Allinsons were there too, and the Paxtons. Burke saw Emily Allinson leave her husband. She walked by the wall of the graveyard. She stared out over the fields to the spot where Mal Trevors had died. She said a few words to Elsie Warden as she passed her by. The two women then looked at Burke for a moment. They laughed. Then Elsie went on her way. Mrs Paxton tried to stay away from both of them. But Mrs Allinson went to her and laid a hand on her arm. The hand held Mrs Paxton in place. Mrs Allinson then leaned down to talk to her.

"What do you think that's about, sir?" asked Stokes.

"A little friendly greeting, perhaps?"

"Doesn't look too friendly to me."

"No, it doesn't, does it? Perhaps we need to have another talk with Mrs Paxton."

By now, Dr Allinson had joined them.

"Any progress?" he asked.

"Slow and steady," said Burke. He felt a stab of guilt as he recalled his dream of the doctor's wife.

"I hear you stirred up the Wardens."

"They've told people about our visit?"

"The mother has spoken of little else. She seems to think you're rude. She says that someone needs to teach you a lesson. I'd watch my back if I were you, Inspector."

"I have Sergeant Stokes here to watch my back," said Burke. "It leaves me free to watch other people."

Allinson grinned. "Good. I don't want to be your doctor as well."

"Tell me," said Burke. "Does your wife know a little of medicine?"

"Many doctors' wives do. Mrs Allinson is trained as a midwife. She has other skills too. She knows what to do in the event of a crisis."

"The women of the village are lucky to have her, then," said Burke. "Very lucky indeed."

The rest of the day added little to what they already knew. They talked to all those who had been at the inn on the night of Mal Trevors's death. They also talked to many who were not there. Few had a good word to say about the dead man. By the end of the day, they were no closer to finding his killer. Burke and Stokes went back to the inn. Burke whispered something to his sergeant, then went to his own room. He stayed there for the rest of the evening.

In time, he must have fallen asleep. The room was darker when he opened his eyes. The inn was quiet. He was not even sure why he had awoken. Then he heard voices speaking softly outside his window. Burke left his bed and walked to the glass. Two women stood in the yard below. In the dim light he could make out the faces of Emily Allinson and Mrs Paxton. The women seemed to be arguing. He could see Mrs Allinson stabbing her finger at the smaller, darker Mrs Paxton. Burke could not make out their words. Then Mrs Allinson turned and walked away. Seconds later, Mrs Paxton followed. By then Burke was on his way downstairs. He left the inn and followed the two women. They took the road that led out of the village. They were heading toward the Paxtons' house. As soon as Mrs Paxton caught up with Mrs Allinson, they left the road and made their way across the fields. They seemed to be heading for the fence on which Mal Trevors had died. Then Burke saw them open a gate in the fence and turn toward the graveyard. The inspector kept himself hidden as best he could. He was helped by the clouds that masked the moon. He was almost at the gate when the women stopped and turned to face him.

"Welcome, Inspector," said Mrs Allinson. She did not look surprised to see him. In fact, Burke thought, she looked rather pleased. He knew then that he had stepped into the trap they had set for him. Mrs Paxton said nothing. She kept her head down. She did not even look in his direction.

Burke heard footsteps behind him. He turned to see Elsie Warden. She was moving slowly through the grass. Her hands brushed the tips of the weeds as she walked. She stopped when she was about twenty feet from him. Mrs Paxton in turn moved away from Mrs Allinson. Burke now found himself at the centre of a triangle formed by the three women.

"Is this how you put paid to Mal Trevors?" he asked.

"We never laid a hand on Mal Trevors," said Mrs Allinson.

"We didn't have to," said Elsie.

Burke tried to keep turning. He had two of the women in sight at all times. He just hoped that he would be fast enough to prevent an attack by the third.

"There are wounds on your chest, Miss Warden," said Burke.

"And on my scalp," she said. "He fought back. Mal always was quick with his hands."

"So you attacked him?"

"In a way." It was Mrs Allinson.

"I don't understand."

"Oh," said Mrs Allinson. "But you will."

Burke felt the ground move under his feet. He jumped back, afraid of falling into some pit. Over by the graveyard wall, pieces of stone shot a foot into the air. They left three holes where they once lay. He heard a howling sound, like wind in a tunnel. Then something scratched his face. It left parallel wounds across his cheek and nose. He raised his arms to protect himself. But the front of his coat was torn open by unseen claws. He smelled foul breath. He thought that he saw a shimmer in the air, like heat rising from summer ground. Slowly, its form became clearer. Burke saw long, dark hair and the shape of breasts and hips.

Faced with a target, Burke struck. He pounded his fist into the figure before him. His fist stopped for a second, then passed straight through the form. He saw Emily Allinson's head jerk back. Blood spurted from her nose. Burke tried to punch again. But he was hit from behind before he could do so. His scalp was ripped open. He felt warm liquid upon his neck. He tried to rise. His right hand was pulled away from him and forced into the air. A sharp pain ran through three of his fingers. The marks of teeth appeared upon the skin of his knuckles. Over by the fence, he saw Elsie Warden gritting her teeth. Elsie shook her head hard.

The pain in Burke's fingers increased. Then the fingers were torn from Burke's hand. His eyes closed. He prepared to die.

From somewhere in the darkness, he heard a loud noise. It sounded like a gunshot. Then a voice said, "That'll be enough, now."

Burke's eyelids felt heavy. Blood dripped from his head when he finally opened them. Sergeant Stokes stood by the graveyard wall. He held a shotgun in his hands.

You took your bloody time, thought Burke.

He caught sight of the shimmer in the air once again. It still had the shape of a woman. It crawled along the ground towards Sergeant Stokes. Burke tried to warn him, but no words came. Instead, his own head was pulled back by the hair. He felt teeth upon his neck.

Stokes saw the shape when it was

almost upon him. He swung the shotgun around and fired.

For a moment, nothing happened. Then, slowly, Emily Allinson's mouth opened. A great gush of red poured from it. She rocked upon her feet. The front of her green dress grew dark with blood. Burke heard a scream that seemed to come from the ground beneath him. It was echoed in turn by Elsie Warden. His hair was released and he fell to the dirt. He felt a weight upon his back as he was used as a stepping-stone by an unseen form. Burke's left hand reached out and grasped a rock from the ground. With the last of his strength, he rose and brought the rock down on the shape moving across the grass. The stone hit its target. Behind him, Elsie Warden's skull cracked. Her eyes rolled back in her head, and she fell down dead.

Stokes was running toward him now. He reloaded the shotgun as he came. He was watching Mrs Paxton. Her face was filled with horror and disgust. She turned from them and ran across the fields. Stokes shouted after her, warning her to stop.

"Let her go," said Burke. "We know where to find her."

And then he fell back on the ground, unconscious.

Eight

Summer came, and the streets grew bright.

The two men met in a bar close to Paddington. They had not seen each other in many months. It was quiet. The lunchtime drinkers were gone. The evening crowd had yet to come. One man was younger and thinner than the other. He wore a glove on his right hand. The other man placed two beers on the table before them. Then he took a seat against the wall.

"How is the hand, sir?" asked Stokes.

"It hurts a little still," said Burke. "It's odd. I can feel the ends of my fingers, even though they're no longer there. Strange, don't you think?"

Stokes shrugged. "To tell the truth, sir, I don't know any more what's strange and what isn't."

He raised his glass and took a long sip.

"You don't have to call me 'sir' any more, you know," said Burke.

"Doesn't seem natural calling you anything else, sir," said Stokes. "I do miss being called 'sergeant', though. I'm trying to get the missus to call me 'sergeant', just so I can hear it again. She won't do it."

"How is the bank?"

"Quiet," he said. "Don't care much for it, to be honest. Still, it keeps me busy. The money helps."

"Yes, I'm sure it does."

They were silent, then, until Stokes said "You still think we did right, not telling them what we saw?"

"Yes," said Burke. "They wouldn't have believed us, even if we had told them the truth. Mrs Allinson had my blood and skin under her nails. The bite marks on my hand matched those of Elsie Warden. They attacked me. That's what the evidence said. Who were we to disagree with the evidence?"

"Killing unarmed women," said Stokes. "I suppose they had no choice but to make us leave the force."

"No, I suppose not."

Burke looked at his former sergeant. He laid his good hand upon the older man's arm.

"But never forget: you didn't kill a woman. You never fired at a woman, and I never hit one. Let us be clear on that."

Stokes nodded.

"I hear they let the Paxton woman go," he said.

"She supported our story. Without

her, it would have gone much harder for us."

"Doesn't seem right, though."

"She wished a man dead. I don't think she thought that wish would come true. She was with the other women, but she did nothing wrong. Nothing that we can prove, at any rate."

Stokes took another sip from his glass.

"And that poor beggar, Allinson."

"Yes," said Burke. "Poor Allinson." The doctor had taken his own life after his wife's death. He had never tried to blame Stokes or Burke for the part they had played in her killing.

Burke spent most of his time thinking about that night. He now knew more about the Underbury Witches and their leader, Ellen Drury, who burned as she hanged. Possession, the term that Stokes had once used, was one answer to what had happened.

It did not seem enough for Burke. He believed with all his heart that what attacked him came also from within the three women, not just from some outside force.

They finished their drinks, then parted on the street. They made promises to meet again, but they knew that they would not. Burke walked in the direction of Hyde Park. Stokes stopped to buy flowers for his wife. Neither saw the small, dark-haired woman who stood in the shadow of a nearby alley. She watched them closely. The air shimmered around her. A faint smell of roasting meat arose.

Mrs Paxton made her choice.

Slowly, she began to follow Burke toward the park.

OPEN DOOR SERIES

SERIES FOUR

The Story of Joe Brown by Rose Doyle
Stray Dog by Gareth O'Callaghan
The Smoking Room by Julie Parsons
World Cup Diary by Niall Quinn
Fair-Weather Friend by Patricia Scanlan
The Quiz Master by Michael Scott

SERIES FIVE

Mrs Whippy by Cecelia Ahern
The Underbury Witches by John Connolly
Mad Weekend by Roddy Doyle
Not a Star by Nick Hornby
Secrets by Patricia Scanlan
Behind Closed Doors by Sarah Webb

TRADE/CREDIT CARD ORDERS TO:
CMD, 55A Spruce Avenue,
Stillorgan Industrial Park,
Blackrock, Co. Dublin, Ireland.
Tel: (+353 1) 294 2560
Fax: (+353 1) 294 2564

TO PLACE PERSONAL/EDUCATIONAL
ORDERS OR TO ORDER A CATALOGUE
PLEASE CONTACT:
New Island, 2 Brookside,
Dundrum Road, Dundrum,
Dublin 14, Ireland.
Tel: (+353 1) 298 6867/298 3411
Fax: (+353 1) 298 7912
www.newisland.ie